I Was Beheaded

I Was Beheaded

P.A. (Sunny) Aslam

I WAS BEHEADED

iUniverse books may be ordered through booksellers or by contacting:

iUniverse
1663 Liberty Drive
Bloomington, IN 47403
www.iuniverse.com
844-349-9409

Because of the dynamic nature of the Internet, any web addresses or links contained in this book may have changed since publication and may no longer be valid. The views expressed in this work are solely those of the author and do not necessarily reflect the views of the publisher, and the publisher hereby disclaims any responsibility for them.

Any people depicted in stock imagery provided by Getty Images are models, and such images are being used for illustrative purposes only. Certain stock imagery © Getty Images.

ISBN: 978-1-6632-5037-7 (sc)
ISBN: 978-1-6632-5036-0 (e)

Library of Congress Control Number: 2023913771

Print information available on the last page.

iUniverse rev. date: 07/31/2023

FADE IN:

INT. PENTAGON CONFERENCE ROOM -

Portraits of past presidents adorn the walls. The front end of the room is overtaken by an interior garden with a banana tree in the middle. A large conference table stands in the middle of the room.

Sitting at the head of the table is VICE PRESIDENT DICK CHENEY. To his right is DEPUTY SECRETARY PAUL WOLFOWITZ. On the other side of Wolfowitz is PROFESSOR MARK FIRST CUTTER. To Cheney's left is ADMIRAL JOHN DOE SINISTER. Next to Sinister is PROFESSOR REPEAT HIS.

                    CHENEY
          Gentlemen, our job is to come up with
          solutions. We haven't found any weapons of
          mass destruction. More Americans are dying
          there. More people are being kidnapped.

The door to the conference room opens. NUKIE PERSON, 34, brunette, in a tight dress walks stiffly into the room and proceeds to the garden. She draws a shiny sword from her holster and, with a swing, cuts the banana tree in two.

His and Cutter startle. Cheney smiles at Nukie

CHENEY

Yes, Nukie, decapitation. When people are kidnapped, they end up cut at the neck

WOLFOWITZ

Nukie, be careful with that sword.

Nukie nods.

HIS

Yes, historically, decapitation has been very instructive and effective.

SINISTER

We are reeling from its effects. We need something to counteract it.

CUTTER

Medical research is trying to help you, Mr. Vice President. We now have the **RESURRECT** Program. The program stands for **re**acting to **surr**eal **e**xecution techniques.

CHENEY

Resurrection is a good word. It means God is on our side. That will help. What exactly are you doing with it?

CUTTER

We are doing a series of experiments on animals to study the effects of decapitation and figure out how to salvage them afterward.

HIS

(laughingly)

There are lot of them walking around in the capitol without heads, even without decapitation.

CHENEY

Good luck with that. You know, we have some fellas in Gitmo who need your experiments.

CUTTER

We have not reached that stage of testing yet. Currently, we are gluing the cut animals back together. We have had success in worms and some invertebrates.

CHENEY

That's great.

CUTTER

But there hasn't been much luck with mice. We are now trying to stitch the heads back on.

CHENEY

How's that going?

CUTTER

Our results are getting better. We can salvage about 50 percent.

CHENEY

That's super.

SINISTER

We have other programs, Vice President. For example, our **IRS** Program—

CHENEY

What is that?

SINISTER

Iraq **r**attlesnake **s**trikes. It is a very innovative, low-tech program that will use rattlesnakes to keep terrorists in check at night, when they usually come out to kill our boys.

CHENEY
(smiling)

Rattlesnakes in uniform for us?

NUKIE

Sort of like using dogs to sniff out bombs.
Very effective. Here rattlesnakes will strike
at jihadists.

CHENEY

Great! Sounds very innovative. I'll give credit
for that to the DOD.

SINISTER

Rattlesnakes come out at night, and we will
put the fear of rattlesnakes into the jihadists.
Rattlesnake bites will not put them in heaven,
according to Islam.

HIS
(laughingly)
Historically, rattlesnakes have rattled many
people.

CHENEY

How are you going to get them there?

WOLFOWITZ

I know DOD has a contract out for testing the concept—a good one.

SINISTER

The Blackwater Company has a research division looking at these rattlesnakes from Texas, mambas from South Africa, and cobras from India. They are in Saudi Arabia and Texas, being trained by experts.

CHENEY

Any success in the field?

SINISTER

Blackwater thinks so. They have Evangelicals who fearlessly handle the rattlesnakes and are training the people and snakes for use in Iraq. Blackwater also has snake charmers from India and tribal shamans from Africa—all working hard. I believe they had quite a bit of success with the rattlers.

CHENEY

Long live rattlers!

NUKIE

We also have the RST Program, which is top
secret.

CHENEY

What is RST?

NUKIE

The Repackage Sex for Terrorists Program.
This will use multimedia platforms and our
burgeoning porn industry to lure terrorists
out of Iraq.

CHENEY

Why are you fellas doing that?

NUKIE

In our research, we noticed that some of the
9/11 terrorists went to strip clubs before they
hijacked the planes.

CHENEY

Sex the jihad way!

SINISTER

We also noticed a great demand for porno movies in Saudi Arabia and the Middle East. Why not package sex for our use?

HIS

(laughingly)

Why not? The role of sex is immense in our history.

CHENEY

Why not indeed? Just make sure this does not get into the news. They don't have the same outlook. They don't believe we have to use all smart means to conquer these people.

WOLFOWITZ

They sure don't.

Everyone nods.

CHENEY

So how are you going to do this? By deploying strippers and promoting a porn division in the army?

HIS

(laughingly)

I can imagine a promotional ad for the deployment of strippers—a **PDS** Program in a **PDF file.**

WOLFOWITZ

(laughingly)

One billion dollars of our slush fund has been allocated for it—a well-endowed program.

CHENEY

How did you ask for the funds?

WOLFOWITZ

It's in there—in the Act to Promote Proper Technology. Just one billion out of one hundred billion.

NUKIE

The army is actively involved in recruiting. They aren't having any difficulty getting these people!

CHENEY

I bet they aren't, but I can see trouble with implementation. Fellows don't mess up. Our heads are on the line.

Everyone smiles.

HIS
(smiling)

Historically, nothing succeeds more than salaciousness.

NUKIE

We are also testing another program called **IDBT**.

CHENEY

What is **IDBT**?

NUKIE

IDBT means Intercontinental Detection and Blow with Turbines. This program will sweep the feet off any terrorists from Syria, Saudi Arabia, or Iran who come through the border, using intercontinental-missile-detection technology and turbines! The turbines will blow them off with air.

CHENEY

Who is behind this?

NUKIE

Boeing and our Jet Propulsion Laboratory. They have a prototype that they tested on our Mexican border. It uses the new "Lou Dobbs" technology. In simple terms, it blast them with hot air.

HIS

(laughingly)

Nothing like hot air to counteract cold facts.

CHENEY

How practical is that?

SINISTER

It's very promising technology. You can put a motion detector on a satellite and then focus it on the borders of Iraq. So when there is movement across the border, the satellite will detect it. Then turbines will blow them away with hot wind.

CHENEY

How much will this cost the taxpayers?

SINISTER

The estimated cost is in the tens of billions, but the technology can also be used on the US-Mexico border. That is why it is named the Lou Dobbs technique. There is plenty of support for it.

WOLFOWITZ

Sounds very doable. I'm always amazed at the brain power in the Pentagon. Nukie, I want to talk to you after the meeting.

NUKIE

Ok, Paul.

FADE TO:

INT. TV STUDIO —

PUBLIC TELLALL VISIONARY faces forward. A sign on the television screen in the background reads, "The Evening News with Public Tellall Visionary."

PUBLIC

First, today's news. In Iraq, President Allavi was declared the winner of the Iraqi election after the recount. The declaration was marred by the attempted assassination of President Allavi. President Bush congratulates the Pentagon for the achievement of successfully reattaching a decapitated robot's head by military doctors at Walter Reed Hospital in a virtual reality simulation. Details after the news. Deputy Secretary Wolfowitz won the Macarthur Genius Award alongside Howard Dean. The education secretary mandates the laminated display of the No Child Left Behind Act in every school as a necessary first step to qualify for the restitution law for schools with many children expelled.

Public turns and faces DR. NERDY SURGEON in surgical garb. Behind them, the television screen switches to a picture of a doctor and nurse tending to a robot.

PUBLIC

Dr. Nerdy Surgeon is the chief of neurosurgery at Mt. Sinai Hospital and an accomplished researcher of reconnective neurosurgery. Thanks for being here.

DR. SURGEON

Glad to be here.

PUBLIC

What do you think of the accomplishments from the doctors at Walter Reed Hospital?

DR. SURGEON

I think they're very significant. They have confirmed our own research with the fruit fly, *Drosophila melanogaster,* where the ability to decapitate and recapitate are perfectly possible. We were working on the lowly nematode *Caenorhabditis elegans* when the Pentagon jumped the gun and ordered a feasibility study of the ten-billion-dollar huma-robot. Our research was a top-secret project until their study was announced.

PUBLIC

Do you think this would work on human beings?

DR. SURGEON

I have no doubt this will be possible in the twenty-first century. We are already able to transplant kidneys, livers, pancreas, intestines, and faces. It is just a quantum jump to reattaching heads. If we can reattach the head of a complicated ten-billion-dollar robot, I am sure we can do it to less complicated *Homo sapiens*, particularly in the developing world, where life is cheap.

PUBLIC

Do you think it's ethical to reattach a head after it was cut off? Will that bring in some changes? I have heard that people who had near-death experiences are profoundly changed by them.

DR. SURGEON

That is an interesting question! For now, we don't have enough evidence to answer it. There was a randomized double-blind trial among neurosurgeons, and the conclusion was that it was perfectly ethical to reattach heads. In this experiment—which was underpowered—statistically the p-value was barely significant. But in these times, that's not an obstacle. Of course, this was a virtual simulation, so the only questions are from ethicists, which aren't that important now. We can get an exception because of the terror threat and 9/11. The only trouble that the military got into was with their indication for decapitation. Of course, with Bush's Doctrine of Terror, we can get permission to go against any pre-9/11 prohibition.

PUBLIC

Could you go into some of the details of what you call *recapitation*?

DR. SURGEON

Yes, that is a new word—a twenty-first century word! Think of taking the cap off a Coca-Cola bottle and putting it back. This is conceptually very similar. Although decapitation was pretty common in the early part of the first millennium and still the method of capital punishment in Saudi Arabia, the need to reattach heads became a necessity due to the Iraq War. In medicine, it is not a new concept. With recapitation, the first part of the body to be reattached is the spinal cord. Of course, the blood supply to the brain needs to be clamped, and any undue blood loss needs to be corrected. We have found that depending on the time elapsed, the regenerated brain can get the stored information back. The first things lost are religious convictions, then moral convictions. This opens up interesting possibilities; one could decapitate people and change their religious convictions! The Bush administration was very interested in that information.

PUBLIC

Has anyone else worked on this idea?

DR. SURGEON

Defense Secretary Rumsfeld and Deputy Secretary Wolfowitz have encouraged the study. They are true visionaries. Since the ethical implications are quite heady, they have outsourced the study to Guantanamo Base.

PUBLIC

Why Guantanamo Base?

Dr. Surgeon smiles.

DR. SURGEON

Well, let me put it this way—there is headroom for experiments in Guantanamo.

Public smiles.

PUBLIC

I see. What other experiments are being conducted there?

DR. SURGEON

Quite exciting things. As you know, war always brings advances in medicine. Remember how the British leapfrogged the development of penicillin during the Second World War? Our military is using billions of your tax dollars in innovative research. For example, the **ESHIT** Project.

Public smiles again.

PUBLIC

ESHIT Project?

DR. SURGEON

It is of momentous importance in transforming humanity.

PUBLIC

Can you tell me a little about it?

DR. SURGEON

I cannot divulge all the details, but the project is called Eliminate Food Side Products, Help, Indulge, and Transform or **ESHIT** for short. It will eliminate the necessity to go to the restroom!

PUBLIC

Really?

DR. SURGEON

Yes, that is the beauty of it! Now the Pentagon won't have to provide latrines for our bravest! They can spend more of their fifteen-month rotation doing actual fighting. Statisticians have estimated that the time saved is substantial.

PUBLIC

Can you explain to the audience how this could be accomplished?

DR. SURGEON

I don't want to go into the details here, but we can short-circuit the human plumbing system and fully utilize the food ingested. The details are military top-secret for now.

PUBLIC

I see.

DR. SURGEON

ESHIT will literally eliminate shit from our vocabulary. We have eliminated this from huma-robots, and preliminary studies at Guantanamo have shown this is possible in people.

PUBLIC

Doctor, is such human experimentation reviewed by an institutional review board or a committee before it is done?

DR. SURGEON

That is the beauty of war; we are able to suspend our ethics. That's what 9/11 has taught us. Terrorist do not have any ethics. They decapitate and indulge in suicide bombs. We can at least try to eliminate their shit and reattach their heads.

PUBLIC

Has the inspector general at the Pentagon and the Justice Department reviewed your positions?

DR. SURGEON

We have great support from faith-based groups and Attorney General Gonzales. Faith-based groups are going to have their Evangelical brethren in congress sponsor the Act to Recap the Decap Bill.

Public and Dr. Surgeon massage their necks and make sure they are still attached properly.

FADE TO:

INT.

DEFENSE SECRETARY RUMSFELD looks in a mirror while shaving. He interrupts his shaving to sing and dance to a song

> RUMSFELD
>
> "Lamination is an abomination / And a disgrace to humankind. / A rumination and summation: / Lamination is an abomination / Inevitable as garbage and poop, / Irresistible to pedagogues / As fundamentalism to conservatives. / Lamination is an abomination / As graffiti in the restroom, / A preservation of pickled ideas, / An irritation and impersonation, / A pedagogical overkill. / Lamination is an abomination. / Retribution to evolution, / An attempt at immortalization. / Prejudices masquerading as art. / Lamination is an abomination, / Pollution, and an irritation.

/ Environmental contamination / Of questionable propagation. / Lamination is an abomination, / A preservation of moral obfuscation, / An attempt at mummification, / An eyesore of memorialization. / Lamination is an abomination, / A pontification, an indemnification, / A skeletonization, a beatification, / A crucifixion of self-evaluation. / Lamination is an abomination. / No consolation to souls of opposite persuasion / For pedagogues of different coloration, / Of ideologues of different ruminations. / Alas it is a Montesorification / For prevention of discoloration. / A preservation of self-preservation / For pedagogues of every persuasion. / To anti-lamination, / My salutation, my summation, / My appreciation, my congratulation—"

A phone rings, interrupting Rumsfeld. He picks it up and presses the accept button.

RUMSFELD

(into phone)

Hello, Rummy here. Is this Wolfie?

(beat)

You found weapons of mass destruction in
Iran?

(beat)

Great! I knew it! I knew it!

WOLFOWITZ

(into phone)

Yes, our scientist in residence at the DOD has
seen a weapon of mass destruction. He did
studies at Walter Reed and Guantanamo. He
swears that if we put the E. coli from Saddam
Hussein's shit in the food supply, it will have
the potential to kill everybody in the world.
It's not a nuclear device, but our scientists
from the Center for Disease Control in
Atlanta are willing to certify it as a WMD.

INTERCUT with

RUMSFELD

Look, I'm not looking for a joking session.
Our heads will roll if we don't find WMDs.

WOLFOWITZ

I hoped a little humor would keep you
grounded. But there is something more
interesting and fascinating. We have some
research telling us that if somebody has been
decapitated, they can be recapitated.

RUMSFELD

What is recapitation?

WOLFOWITZ

It's the reattachment of a decapitated head.

RUMSFELD

Goodness gracious!

WOLFOWITZ

Research is now at the stage where robots can be decapitated and then recapitated.

RUMSFELD

How does that help us? I take it back. We have some robotic politicians.

WOLFOWITZ

I wish I could decapitate some of them.

RUMSFELD

(singing)

"Decapitation is an incapacitation / Fit for army's meditation. / I have great trepidation / For its consideration."

WOLFOWITZ

But, Rummy, there is one more interesting thing in the pipeline. Did you listen to what our research produced on the newscast yesterday? According to the neurosurgeon at Mt. Sinai Hospital, it is possible to recap the decapitated heads of animals already. What's interesting is that in the future, the army could recapitate decapitated people. Secondly, we could change their religious convictions.

RUMSFELD

Goodness gracious! Now Islamists have dug their own decapitation hole.

(singing)

"Decapitation, your decapitation, / For your edification, / For your consideration. / Can be a matter of religious enlightenment, / And matter of the justifiable punishment / For terrorist at Guantanamo. / For by your recapitation, / You will receive your salvation. / What an astonishing consideration. / What a mortifying euphemism."

WOLFOWITZ

(singing)

"God and heritage foundation, / Our heads and religion / Come in syncopation, / In mutual admiration."

RUMSFELD

Things are looking up. How can we use this?

WOLFOWITZ

We can set up a decapitation camp at Guantanamo. Let's get the surgeon from Mt. Sinai and NIH involved.

(laughingly)

Once they have their technique standardized, we can get some of the jihadists to volunteer for the decapitation. Then we can recapitate them and drop them in the Middle East, where they will be our spies.

RUMSFELD

This will require authorization from the very top.

WOLFOWITZ

I'm pretty sure we can talk Dick into approving it.

RUMSFELD

Let me call him right now. Stay on the line.

We'll have a conference call

Rumsfeld entered Cheney's number into his phone.

The phone rings. Cheney grabs it and presses the accept button.

CHENEY

(Into phone)

Hello, Rummy. What's up?

INTERCUT with

RUMSFELD

(Into phone)

We've hit the jackpot!

CHENEY

You found weapons of mass destruction?

RUMSFELD

Dick, Wolfie is also on the line. He has the news.

WOLFOWITZ

(into phone)

Dick, we have a scientist at the DOD who will swear That the E. coli strain cultured from Saddam Hussein's shit is capable of killing everybody in the world. The CDC in Atlanta is willing to certify that. We can put out the story that this is more potent than a nuclear device! Saddam is carrying it; only he is immune to it. He can surreptitiously spread it to everybody and kill them. You know, by handshakes and dipping a finger in food.

CHENEY

Are you serious?

WOLFOWITZ

You can sell it to the American public with very little spin. We have some capital.

Cheney smirks.

CHENEY

You people are full of shit.

RUMSFELD

That's what I told Wolfie, but he has some better news.

WOLFOWITZ

Our top-secret research on how to reattach decapitated heads has borne fruit. We were able to reattach jihadist heads in Guantanamo. DOD scientists noted that once they reattached the heads, their religious beliefs changed.

CHENEY

Religion changes?

WOLFOWITZ

Apparently so. Some jihadists became Zionists.

CHENEY

(laughingly)

We have achieved a moral victory of sorts.

All three laugh and high-five.

FADE TO:

INT. SORI ROOM —

SENATOR CHUCK SCHUMER bangs his gavel, starting the session. Rumsfeld smiles. SENATOR ORRIN HATCH and SENATOR FEINSTEIN

SENATOR SCHUMER

I want to welcome Defense Secretary Rumsfeld. Please, what's going on in the virtual reality world in Iraq?

RUMSFELD

We have exciting things going on at the Pentagon. In virtual reality, we have been able to conquer the act of decapitation.

Rumsfeld starts playing a video of a robot's decapitation and recapitation.

RUMSFELD (CONT'D)

This video here is of the decapitation of a robot and its recapitation

SENATOR SCHUMER

What is recapitation?

RUMSFELD

It's putting the head back on the shoulders, in a literal sense.

SENATOR SCHUMER

(sarcastically)

I'm glad the Pentagon is learning how to put a head back on its shoulders.

RUMSFELD

We have now become experts. If you look at this—

Rumsfeld points to the video. There is laughter throughout the room.

SENATOR SCHUMER

Please go on.

RUMSFELD

I have brought the famous surgeon and researcher, Professor Mark First Cutter, who will explain the intricacies of recapitation to you.

Cutter is sworn in.

CUTTER

(Reading from notes)

I am indeed privileged to report to you the great progress made in the science of decapitation and recapitation by the researchers of the National Institute of Health. With the help and support of Defense Secretary Rumsfeld and Deputy Secretary Wolfowitz, we have accomplished the first decapitation and recapitation of a huma-robot.

SENATOR SCHUMER

Professor, what use does the DOD have for this decapitation and recapitation business?

CUTTER

For obvious reasons, I'm not going to describe the decapitation process, and recapitation is a DOD secret. What I can say in public testimony, though, is that recapitation is the reattachment of a decapitated head.

SENATOR SCHUMER

What good is it, spending one hundred million dollars to find out that you can reattach a robot's decapitated head?

CUTTER

There are many benefits. In the virtual reality world, Senator Schumer, when a decapitated huma-robot is recapitated, it can—it seems—change its religious orientation.

SENATOR SCHUMER

So you are saying that an Islamic robot can be made into a fundamentalist Judeo-Christian robot?

CUTTER

Exactly.

SENATOR SCHUMER

I hear rumors that the sexual orientation of the robot can also be changed.

CUTTER

Correct.

SENATOR SCHUMER

Secretary Rumsfeld, what—in DOD's view— should the sexual orientation of the robots be?

RUMSFELD

In the military, we believe it should not be gay.

SENATOR SCHUMER

Is the Bush administration deciding the sexual orientation of robots?

RUMSFELD

The Justice Department has discussed the subject in detail. They have concluded that in the US constitution, there are no rights for gay robots. Accordingly, that is the President Bush's position, and he has the right to write directives. According to conservative Christian theology, one should eliminate the gay condition in robots. It should be nipped in the bud.

SENATOR SCHUMER

That is atrocious. The Senate and this committee will sponsor a resolution to oppose President Bush's position.

RUMSFELD

I'm sorry, Senator. President Bush has said that he will veto any such resolution.

SENATOR SCHUMER

Now I ask Senator Orrin Hatch from Utah to continue the questioning.

SENATOR HATCH

(To Rumsfeld)

I congratulate you on the news you have brought. This is a real breakthrough. As you know, I'm all for religious freedom. Islamic fundamentalism is something else.

RUMSFELD

I agree with you completely, Senator. Islamic fundamentalism breeds terror.

SENATOR HATCH

Professor Cutter how is that you can program a change in sexual orientation into a decapitated robot.

CUTTER

The details are top secret. In short, a click of the mouse is all that is necessary

SENATOR HATCH

That is stupendous! Can you extrapolate the information that you gained during this research and apply it to humans? If so, how?

CUTTER

We have some data from South Korea that suggests it's possible in fruit flies and also round worms. We have even come close in some humans that we recovered after decapitation. However, details cannot be divulged at this venue.

SENATOR HATCH

That's great! That's great! Get the research going, boys! I yield the rest of my time.

SENATOR SCHUMER

Senator Feinstein from California.

SENATOR FEINSTEIN

Professor Cutter, who authorized this research?

CUTTER

This was a special project that was promoted by the Pentagon and endorsed by the highest levels.

SENATOR FEINSTEIN

Carl Rove or the president?

The senators in the room laugh.

SENATOR FEINSTEIN (CONT'D)

Where is the legal basis for trying to change sexual orientation?

RUMSFELD

We had Secretary Gonzales look into it, and he wrote a legal brief.

SENATOR FEINSTEIN

I believe it's atrocious and unconstitutional to change the sexual orientation of robots. This shows how heartless the Bush administration is. Just because the robots do not have a voting constituency. Mark my words—that will change.

RUMSFELD

Senator, we have brought our ethicist in residence, Mr. Ethic Knowall, who will answer your concerns.

ETHIC KNOWALL enters the room.

SENATOR SCHUMER

Mr. Knowall, raise your right hand

Knowall raises his right hand and is sworn in.

SENATOR SCHUMER (CONT'D)

What is your background?

KNOWALL

I am a minister, a tele-evangelist, and an advocate for religion in the malls.

SENATOR SCHUMER

How did you come to the DOD?

KNOWALL

By divine intervention.

SENATOR SCHUMER

I'm not getting it.

KNOWALL

I was sitting down one day, when I got a call from Secretary Rumsfeld. He felt I could do the job.

SENATOR SCHUMER

I see.

KNOWALL

I feel that was divinely ordained.

SENATOR SCHUMER

What do you think about the sexual orientation of robots?

KNOWALL

I believe that since the robots were born without sex, they should not have any sexual orientation.

SENATOR SCHUMER

Are you going to deny the robots' fundamental right to sexual orientation?

KNOWALL

In our constitution, there is nothing written about robots. The government can make its own rules and stick it to the robots.

SENATOR SCHUMER

I see, you have a philosophy of sticking it to robots. What is your opinion of human experimentation on Guantanamo prisoners?

KNOWALL

I believe that terrorists are not human beings. I think they are the work of Satan. They will burn in hell for all eternity. They have no rights.

SENATOR SCHUMER

Have you heard of the Geneva Convention?

KNOWALL

The Geneva Agreement has no validity after 9/11.

SENATOR SCHUMER

What is your opinion on decapitating prisoners?

KNOWALL

If terrorists decapitate soldiers and American contractors, we don't have to worry about decapitating terrorists.

SENATOR SCHUMER

Suppose they were innocent.

KNOWALL

That's too bad. The US Army cannot do anything bad.

SENATOR SCHUMER

Do you think you can think objectively? Despite being engaged by the DOD, can you think of an individual separately from the interests of the DOD?

KNOWALL

I believe I'm looking after the real interests of those terrorists. I want them to get salvation. It looks like the only way they can get salvation is by decapitation and recapitation.

SENATOR SCHUMER

As an ethicist first, can you judge people from different camps? Do you understand what I'm asking, Mr. Knowall?

KNOWALL

I believe there is only one God's ethics, and

that's ours.

Senator Schumer bangs his gavel.

SENATOR SCHUMER

The committee is adjourned for now.

Photographers rush in and take pictures of the senators.

FADE TO:

INT. NUKE ALL HEADQUARTERS/MAIN OFFICE —

Nukie and Wolfowitz sit at a desk.

NUKIE

(singing)

"The decapitation is / A surprising solution

/ For nuclear person, / Because it treats, /

Capitol hemophilia. / Decapitation is /

Homo purification, / Even for huma-robot.

/ Decapitated head, / I can change your /
Homo-orientation."

WOLFOWITZ

You have a good voice, Nukie. Look at that!
What serendipity! We tried to encourage
some real research, and what did we get? A
decapitation—a masterpiece! There is so
much promise in the research for recapitation.
Can you imagine how many people we can
satisfy via recapitation? First, of course, we
have to do the decapitation.

NUKIE

(still singing)

Paul, Paul, "Decapitation, decapitation, /
What an abomination. / What a deft stroke!
/ What a masterly flash!"

Nukie takes out her sword and swings it.

NUKIE (CONT'D)

"Recapitation, recapitation / What a sliver line in the head. / A silver lining of decapitation / And a golden reorientation. / Let us laminate the decapitation, / The research on recapitation. / Let us fast-track virtual reality / Into human sexuality, homo reality."

(Speaking normally)

Paul, apart from the official line, what do you think about homosexuality?

WOLFOWITZ

Nukie, I believe homosexuality is an aberration. Something must have gone astray when the brain was developing.

NUKIE

I think there is a lot of truth to your idea. Otherwise, why would Judeo- Christian-Islamic holy books all slam it?

WOLFOWITZ

That's exactly on target. I believe homosexuality is an acquired lifestyle.

NUKIE

You think it's a corrupted lifestyle?

WOLFOWITZ

That's my idea. Why would an individual try such an aberrant sexual intercourse otherwise? Why do all holy books prohibit it?

NUKIE

I suppose so. The mixture of personal choice and sexuality is a complicated matter.

WOLFOWITZ

You're absolutely right. In my case, the trouble I'm having with my wife reflects that mix. After seeing eye-to-eye for many years, to not to do so is tough.

NUKIE

I'm sorry to hear you're having trouble with your marriage.

WOLFOWITZ

Yes, I'm having major trouble. In fact, I'm almost separated.

NUKIE

I'm sorry to hear that.

The phone rings. Nukie grabs it.

NUKIE
(into phone)
Hello, Jay.
(beat)
What did you say? Cheney what?
(beat)
Cheney disappeared from a secure location in Iraq?
(to Wolfowitz)
Did you know about this?

WOLFOWITZ

I knew he was going to Iraq on a secret mission.

NUKIE

(into phone)

Jay, where did you get this information?

(beat)

Reuters is telling you that Cheney disappeared from a secure location in Iraq? My god, can there be any worse news?

Nukie hangs up the phone.

WOLFOWITZ

Who was on the phone, Nukie?

NUKIE

My good friend Jay Reporter, a reporter for the *New York Times*.

WOLFOWITZ

You know Jay Reporter?

NUKIE

Jay has been a friend of mine since college.

What do you think of the news?

WOLFOWITZ

I'm inclined not to believe it. I'll have to call
and find out.

Wolfowitz reaches for the phone.

FADE TO:

INT. TV STUDIO —

Public faces the audience. Next to him sits JAY REPORTER.

PUBLIC

We have learned that Vice President Cheney
is missing while on a secret trip to Iraq.
When he was in the green zone in Baghdad,
apparently, he was kidnapped. To give us
more information on this subject, we have
the roving reporter for the *New York Times*,
Jay Reporter.

JAY

A usually reliable source told us that Vice President Cheney was taken at gunpoint by some Iraqis dressed in army uniforms and driven out in a Hummer. All American troops are on high alert and have been mobilized to search for the vice president. So far, the searches have been unrevealing.

PUBLIC

We've also been told Fox News has reported that Vice President Cheney grabbed an AK-47 and started shooting when he was confronted by the group of insurgents.

JAY

As you know, reports vary. MSNBC reported that when Cheney started shooting, he shot two friendly intelligence agents. Of course, the details are not clear.

PUBLIC

Has anybody taken responsibility for this?

JAY

No group has taken responsibility at this
time.

PUBLIC

To discuss the significance of this event, we
have two people in the studio remotely—
Professor Repeat His, the famous vice-
presidential historian, and Professor High
Spin, a Professor of television at Pepperdine
University.

His and Spin appear on TV monitors.

PUBLIC (CONT'D)

Professors, welcome. Professor His, what do
you think of the news?

HIS

If it is correct, it is indeed bad news. The fact
that Cheney grabbed an AK-47 and tried to
defend himself is highly significant and great
for vice presidential history.

PUBLIC

Professor Spin, what do you make of the news?

SPIN

It shows high courage and a fast trigger finger. The alleged shooting of security people falls in line with his previous behavior. He shot a friend while duck hunting.

PUBLIC

It's unfortunate he shot his own security agents, if it did happen.

HIS

In war, being fast with the trigger is important. The National Rifle Association would be proud. It's unfortunate there was some friendly fire, but Cheney's aura is sure to go up. He's going to be remembered as someone with the greatest imagination and fastest trigger finger.

SPIN

It's remarkable that Cheney was able to grab an AK-47 and shoot. That shows his high mettle. It doesn't matter that he shot his own people. Previously, he was known to shoot from his mouth. There's nothing wrong now that he's becoming famous for shooting from his hip as well. What's important is what happened to him.

PUBLIC

We have just received some breaking news. Jay Reporter, please tell us what you know.

JAY

Apparently, after Cheney shot the security guards guarding him, there was a lot of confusion. The insurgents were able to grab him and drive away in a Hummer. Now several groups are claiming responsibility for his apparent abduction. Of the groups, the Gay Iraqis for Liberation or GIL and the

National Rifle Association for Iraqi (NRI),
Nation are the most credible.

PUBLIC

We are getting information from an
independent news channel, Al Arabiya. They
have reported that Iraqi officials are saying
Cheney would have been saved from abduction
if he had not grabbed the AK-47 and started
shooting. Cheney is now under the protection
of the Gay Iraqis for Liberation.

JAY

I'm now getting reports that the group called
Gay Iraqis for Liberation has called for the
immediate removal of all troops from Iraq.
They have threatened to kill Vice President
Cheney if this is not done.

PUBLIC

Professor His, what do you think of this?

HIS

This is certainly going to make history. Cheney is going to go down in history as the only vice president captured in war who went down shooting.

SPIN

Certainly, he is going to be regarded as man of great vision and a martyr.

JAY

We are now being told that news about Vice President Cheney is circulating through Al Arabiya. GIL has sent a videotape to Al Arabiya, showing Vice President Cheney with his characteristic Mona Lisa smile. There appears to be a dumbbell pierced through his nose. The whole thing is a shock and quite bizarre.

A picture of Cheney with a dumbbell nose piercing and a smile appears on the screen behind Public and Jay.

PUBLIC

Professor His, what do you think of this picture of Cheney with his nose pierced?

HIS

I'm sure future historians will ask questions when they nose around with this information. It's truly remarkable.

SPIN

Indeed, that is a spectacle of the highest order. I hope they gave him some local anesthetic before they put that dumbbell through Cheney's nasal septum.

PUBLIC

Does anybody know about this particular group?

JAY

There is very little known about the group. As you know, Islamists do not approve of any gay group.

PUBLIC

And body piercing?

JAY

Yes, it is bizarre! There is a background song.
(singing)
"Eeny, meeny, Cheney, woe, / Catch a liar by the toe. / If he smirks, let him go. / Eeny, meeny, Cheney, woe."

PUBLIC

Very bizarre!

JAY

"Eeny, meeny, Cheney, woe, / Catch a liar by the toe ...

FADE TO:

INT. TV STUDIO — (LATER)

Public, Jay, Cutter, and Sinister sit in the background.

PUBLIC

This is a special report on Vice President Cheney. We have come to know that the vice president was rescued in a daring raid by marine combatants. Pentagon has put out a special bulletin about Vice President. To tell us about the details of the story, we have Jay Reporter. Jay, please tell us what happened.

JAY

In a daring raid, Vice President Cheney was snatched from the people who abducted him. I want to warn the audience that the details of what happened to the vice president may be shocking.

PUBLIC

We also have Professor Mark First Cutter and Admiral John Doe Sinister from the Pentagon to supply further details.

CUTTER

Vice President Cheney was first seen with a decapitation wound in a mobile operating room in Iraq. Immediately, I was contacted by the Pentagon to perform the recapitation operation that we'd perfected on robots. Since we already had the technology, tele-robotic microsurgery was done.

PUBLIC

What do you mean by tele-robotic microsurgery?

CUTTER

That means you sit in front of your computer and operate using robots attached to instruments in the field. This technology has been available for the last five years. I was able to operate on Vice President Cheney without actually being present in Iraq. I was able to recapitate the vice president.

PUBLIC

Was the operation successful, Doctor?

CUTTER

All indications so far are that it was successful.

PUBLIC

Congratulations! Admiral Sinister, when would Cheney be available for a trans-oceanic appearance on public television?

SINISTER

Vice President Cheney is at a secure location. I cannot divulge the site or the time he would appear.

PUBLIC

Professor Cutter, has this operation been tested on human beings before?

CUTTER

That is a classified matter.

PUBLIC

Now, to throw some light on these events, we have Professor His and Professor Spin.

His and Spin appear on a television screen behind Public.

PUBLIC

Professor His, what is the significance of these events?

HIS

There is no precedent to this momentous event. As you know, the importance of vice precedents is often compared to a container of warm spit.

Public smiles.

PUBLIC

Yes, a container of warm spit! Professor Spin, do you see any significance in Cheney's abduction and the ditty sung by the gay

Islamic group? That's a sophisticated parody, is it not?

The song plays in the background.

SPIN

Yes, that is a sophisticated parody. I think they got help from the liberal media cells in the US

The song plays again.

SPIN (CONT'D)

The resurrection of that song required the liberal media's help.

PUBLIC

Do you really think there is a liberal media cell helping Islamists in Iraq? Are you serious?

SPIN

I'm pretty sure. Vice President Cheney is persona non grata with the liberal media. I think anything is possible.

PUBLIC

Professor His, could Vice President Cheney's comeback be described as a resurrection?

HIS

Yes, this was indeed a resurrection—a resurrection that was verified by the media. A miracle as great as the resurrection of Christ! A resurrection brought on by American ingenuity and the advancement of science. Congratulations, Professor Cutter.

FADE TO:

INT. TV STUDIO —

Public faces a camera. His and Spin sit next to him. SUPERIMPOSE: "Three months later."

PUBLIC

Today I must report a major change in policy from Vice President Cheney. Cheney described the Iraqi policy as needing an about-face change. He now agrees that the Iraqi invasion has brought on unexpected results. He agrees with critics that radical changes are necessary for improvement. He also said that in light of the present mess in Iraq, he would not have gone to war in retrospect! There is some question as to whether this is the administration's view now. The White House spokesman seemed surprised by the vice president's admission and has promised a clarification from President Bush. In order to give us some perspective on these events, we have Professor His and Professor Spin. Professor His, what is your take on Vice President Cheney's comments?

HIS

It is indeed remarkable. Such an admission really is a great surprise. Until now, Vice President Cheney has consistently maintained that going to Iraq was the right thing to do. It seems likely that this change of heart came after a change of head. How much of this is due to the historic recapitation operation? It's difficult to say now. Only time will tell.

PUBLIC

Professor Spin, what is your take on these events?

SPIN

This is, as Churchill said, a triumph and tragedy. The fact that Vice President Cheney was abducted is a tragedy. It is a tragedy of Shakespearean proportions. The fact that he was successfully recapitated by tele-robotic surgery is of Orwellian significance. This also shows the truth of resurrection.

PUBLIC

Thank you, Professors His and Spin.

His and Spin leave the studio.

PUBLIC (CONT'D)

In order to give you political commentary on this, we have two people: Deputy Secretary Wolfowitz, a close associate of the vice president, and Defense Munition, a fellow at the Washington think tank Nuke All.

Wolfowitz and DEFENSE MUNITION enter the studio and sit next to Public.

PUBLIC (CONT'D)

Wolfowitz, what is your take on this?

WOLFOWITZ

This is very unfortunate. Obviously, the reattachment has produced some errors in thinking. Now Vice President Cheney is indulging in liberal fuzzy thinking. What this has demonstrated, according our medical experts, is a slight asymmetry in the neuronal attachments, which has caused difference in opinions. I would prefer the original orientation of Vice President Cheney's head.

PUBLIC

Defense Munition, what do you think?

DEFENSE

This is indeed a triumph and tragedy. This is a Pyrrhic victory. It's great that American medical science was able to reattach Vice President Cheney's head, but unfortunately, the orientation of his thinking has changed. I wonder if the angle of attachment has changed his visual and mental perspectives?

PUBLIC

Thank you, Deputy Secretary Wolfowitz and Defense Munition.

Wolfowitz and Defense leave the studio.

PUBLIC (CONT'D)

Now, to give us more details on this fast-moving story, I have Jay Reporter.

Jay enters the studio and sits next to Public.

PUBLIC (CONT'D)

Jay, please tell us the parallel story that has come through.

JAY

The other part of this story is muted. Vice President Cheney and his wife have provided us with a written statement that Cheney is coming out as the first gay vice president. Mrs. Cheney fully supports this process.

PUBLIC

In order for the nation to get an appropriate idea of Vice President Cheney's viewpoint, he has agreed to be interviewed remotely from his office. Welcome, Vice President!

INT. CHENEY'S OFFICE —

CHENEY

Thanks for having me.

INTERCUT with TV Studio.

PUBLIC

How do you see things after your recent experience in Iraq?

CHENEY

It was a life-changing experience for me.

PUBLIC

I bet it was. How were you treated by the insurgents?

CHENEY

I was tied up and blindfolded, but I was given food and treated well until our government failed to negotiate.

PUBLIC

Why do you think the government failed to negotiate?

CHENEY

(laughingly)

The answer is ideology, stupid.

PUBLIC

(laughingly)

Of course, it is. Then what happened?

CHENEY

I was taken to a room while blindfolded. I could hear people arguing in Arabic.

PUBLIC

Did they tell you about their negotiations with the US government?

CHENEY

They told me no one would talk to them because they were part of the Gay Iraqis for Liberation.

PUBLIC

What happened next?

CHENEY

I was held down, and somebody gave me an injection. I remember it was fast.

PUBLIC

I believe you were rescued at that time. Apparently, you were wounded.

CHENEY

Yes, I was apparently decapitated! The rest is history.

PUBLIC

How was the recovery from your operation?

CHENEY

The recovery was slow and painful. Nothing funny about it.

PUBLIC

Now do you feel well.

CHENEY

I feel perfectly well. My mind is completely clear. I know there's this disinformation campaign saying I'm mentally unbalanced now. Nothing could be further from the truth.

PUBLIC

You've changed your opinion on Iraq?

CHENEY

I was wrong about Iraq. There were no weapons of mass destruction there. I was wrong, and I was obstinate.

PUBLIC

What made you change your mind?

CHENEY

I believe it was my experience. Everything is clear. I had an epiphany!

PUBLIC

An epiphany?

CHENEY

Everything seems clear now. All the cobwebs in my brain have gone.

PUBLIC

Some of your old associates, like Deputy Secretary Wolfowitz, are calling your ideas wrong. They say you've changed your mind because of the operation. Do you have any comments?

CHENEY

Wolfie is an ideologue. He cannot see truth in anything he doesn't believe in. Facts are spun according to his ideology.

PUBLIC

Let me ask you another question. You have put out a statement, saying your sexual orientation has changed.

CHENEY

Yes, that's true; I put out the statement. I think I always had a gay orientation. I always thought my daughter's orientation was an extension of mine. That wasn't new. After my recapitation experience, things became clearer.

PUBLIC

I hear neocons are saying you aren't the same person. In fact, some say you are an impostor.

CHENEY

No, I'm the same person—or almost the same person. My views have changed.

PUBLIC

Thank you very much, Mr. Vice President.

FADE TO:

INT. TV STUDIO —

Public sits at the desk and looks at the camera.

PUBLIC

Since the last interview we had with Vice President Cheney, we have learned that he has been put on house arrest under the allegations of mental instability. Republicans are thinking of bringing in a motion to impeach the vice president. Central intelligence sources have told us that Vice President Cheney may not be the vice president but someone impersonating him. We have to stop there for now. For more details, please visit https://www.pbsgossip.org.

FADE OUT

THE END

Printed in the United States
by Baker & Taylor Publisher Services